D0120329

That Dog!

Level 2C

Written by Sam Hay
Illustrated by Vian Oelofsen

What is synthetic phonics?

Synthetic phonics teaches children to recognise the sounds of letters and to blend 'synthesise' them together to make whole words.

Understanding sound/letter relationships gives children the confidence and ability to read unfamiliar words, without having to rely on memory or guesswork; this helps them progress towards independent reading.

Did you know? Spoken English uses more than 40 speech sounds. Each sound is called a *phoneme*. Some phonemes relate to a single letter (d-o-g) and others to combinations of letters (sh-ar-p). When a phoneme is written down it is called a *grapheme*. Teaching these sounds, matching them to their written form and sounding out words for reading is the basis of synthetic phonics.

Consultant

I love reading phonics has been created in consultation with language expert Abigail Steel. She has a background in teaching and teacher training and is a respected expert in the field of Synthetic Phonics. Abigail Steel is a regular contributor to educational publications. Her international education consultancy supports parents and teachers in the promotion of literacy skills.

Reading tips

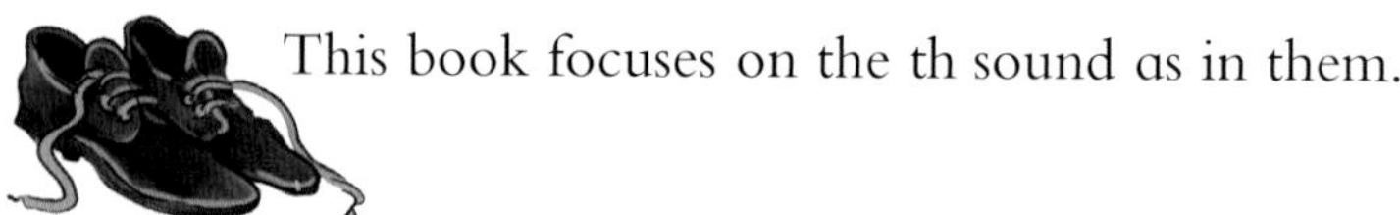

This book focuses on the th sound as in them.

Tricky words in this book

Any words in bold may have unusual spellings or are new and have not yet been introduced.

Tricky words in this book:

the my are to
was said they good

Extra ways to have fun with this book

After the reader has finished the story, ask them questions about what they have just read:

What rescues Tim and Ben?
What mischief does Bob get up to?

Explain that the two letters 'th' make one sound. Think of other words that use the 'th' sound, such as those and that.

I like to read quietly in my bed. Sometimes I read to myself, but mostly I read out loud.

A pronunciation guide

This grid highlights the sounds used in the story and offers a guide on how to say them.

s as in sat	a as in ant	t as in tin	p as in pig	i as in ink
n as in net	c as in cat	e as in egg	h as in hen	r as in rat
m as in mug	d as in dog	g as in get	o as in ox	u as in up
l as in log	f as in fan	b as in bag	j as in jug	v as in van
w as in wet	z as in zip	y as in yet	k as in kit	qu as in quick
x as in box	ff as in off	ll as in ball	ss as in kiss	zz as in buzz
ck as in duck	pp as in puppy	nn as in bunny	rr as in arrow	gg as in egg
dd as in daddy	bb as in chubby	tt as in attic	sh as in shop	ch as in chip
th as in them				

Be careful not to add an ‘uh’ sound to ‘s’, ‘t’, ‘p’, ‘c’, ‘h’, ‘r’, ‘m’, ‘d’, ‘g’, ‘l’, ‘f’ and ‘b’. For example, say ‘fff’ not ‘fuh’ and ‘sss’ not ‘suh’.

Dad is mad. 'That dog got mud on **the** rug!' Mum is fed up. 'That dog sat on **my** hat!'

Tim is sad. ‘Bob is not a bad dog!’

Dad and Tim **are** in the van.
Tim is off **to** camp.

Bob will miss Tim.

Dad and Tim got a shock.
Bob **was** in the van.

‘This is not a dog camp!’ **said** Dad. ‘Sit in the van, bad dog!’

Tim spots his best chum Ben.

Then **they** run up a hill.

But at the top they get lost.

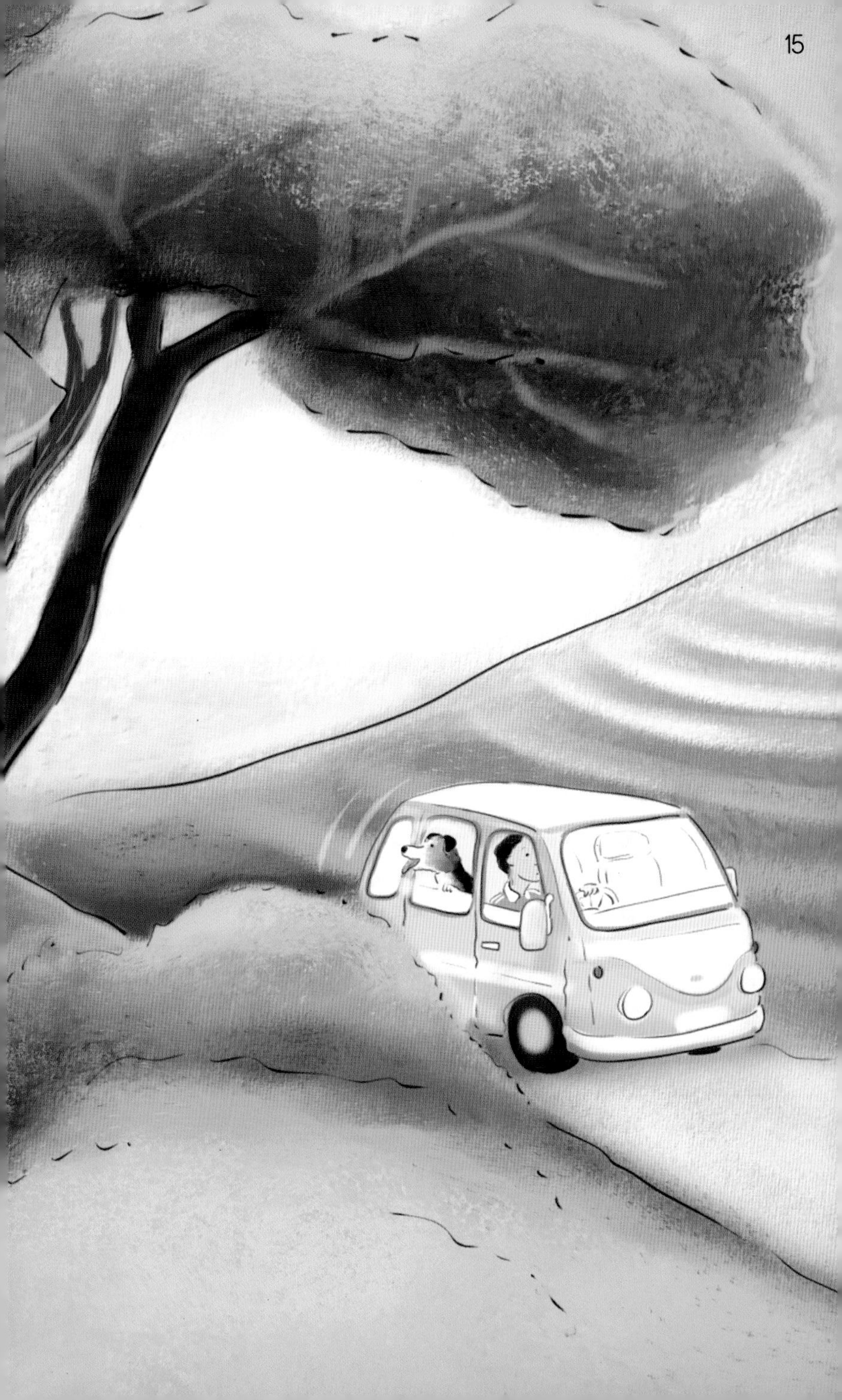

'Dad! Help!' yells Tim.

'Tim?' said Dad.
But Dad cannot spot them.

Then Bob runs up the hill.

Bob spots them!

Tim got a big lick!
'That dog is **good**!' said Dad.

But then Bob spots a bog!

Plop!
Bob is in the bog.

Then Bob runs back to them. 'Yuk!' said Dad. 'That is a bad smell!'

OVER 48 TITLES IN SIX LEVELS
Abigail Steel recommends...

An Hachette UK Company
www.hachette.co.uk

First published in Great Britain in 2012 by TickTock, an imprint of Octopus Publishing Group Ltd, Endeavour House, 189 Shaftesbury Avenue, London WC2H 8JY.
www.octopusbooks.co.uk

ISBN 978 1 84898 388 5

Printed and bound in China
10 9 8 7 6 5 4 3 2